I0757479

OLOKUN OF THE GALAXY
ESTHER IVEREM

ISBN 978-0-692-96820-8 hardcover
     978-0-692-96985-4 ebook

Library of Congress Control Number: 2017916370

The author acknowledges use of public domain images from NASA in creating this book. Thanks to Julian Byfield for assisting with the photo session for Olokun of the Galaxy. Thanks again to Zeph Ernest for creating the image moved to the cover for the third printing. Thanks to Tony Medina and Melissa Tuckey for their advance reviews and Liana Asim and Frank Dexter Brown for their proofing. Thanks to friends and family that have encouraged me with my art, including my late mother Margaret Eleanor Schwartz Curry, Sisters With Intention, Akili Ron Anderson, Januwa Moja, Stephanie Rones, Kendall Dorman and JT. Thanks to all those who have purchased and loved Olokun of the Galaxy dolls and soft sculpture!

Printed and bound in the USA
First printing November 2017
Second printing 2021
Third printing 2024

Published by Seeing Black Press
6323 Georgia Avenue #55943
Washington, DC 20011

www.estheriverem.net

*This book is inspired by Olokun,
an African spirit for the deepest ocean.*

*It is dedicated to the millions
who perished in the Maafa.
And those who survived.*

*To all my ancestors,
named and unnamed,
known and unknown.*

*To Mazi. And all those in
generations yet to come who will
need to save themselves and humanity.*

*To all those working for
a world with renewable
energy and renewed ecosystems
and oceans.*

*To Michael Byfield,
because he has a heart big enough
to care about the whole
world and universe.*

The ocean does not remember a time
When Olokun did not exist in its belly.
And Olokun does not remember a time
When the ocean was not home.

Olokun was born in the same moments when
Falling rain first filled the earth's deepest trenches.
Then floors, valleys, basins and continental shelves.
Creating vast oceans, filling Earth
With first the possibility of life—and death.

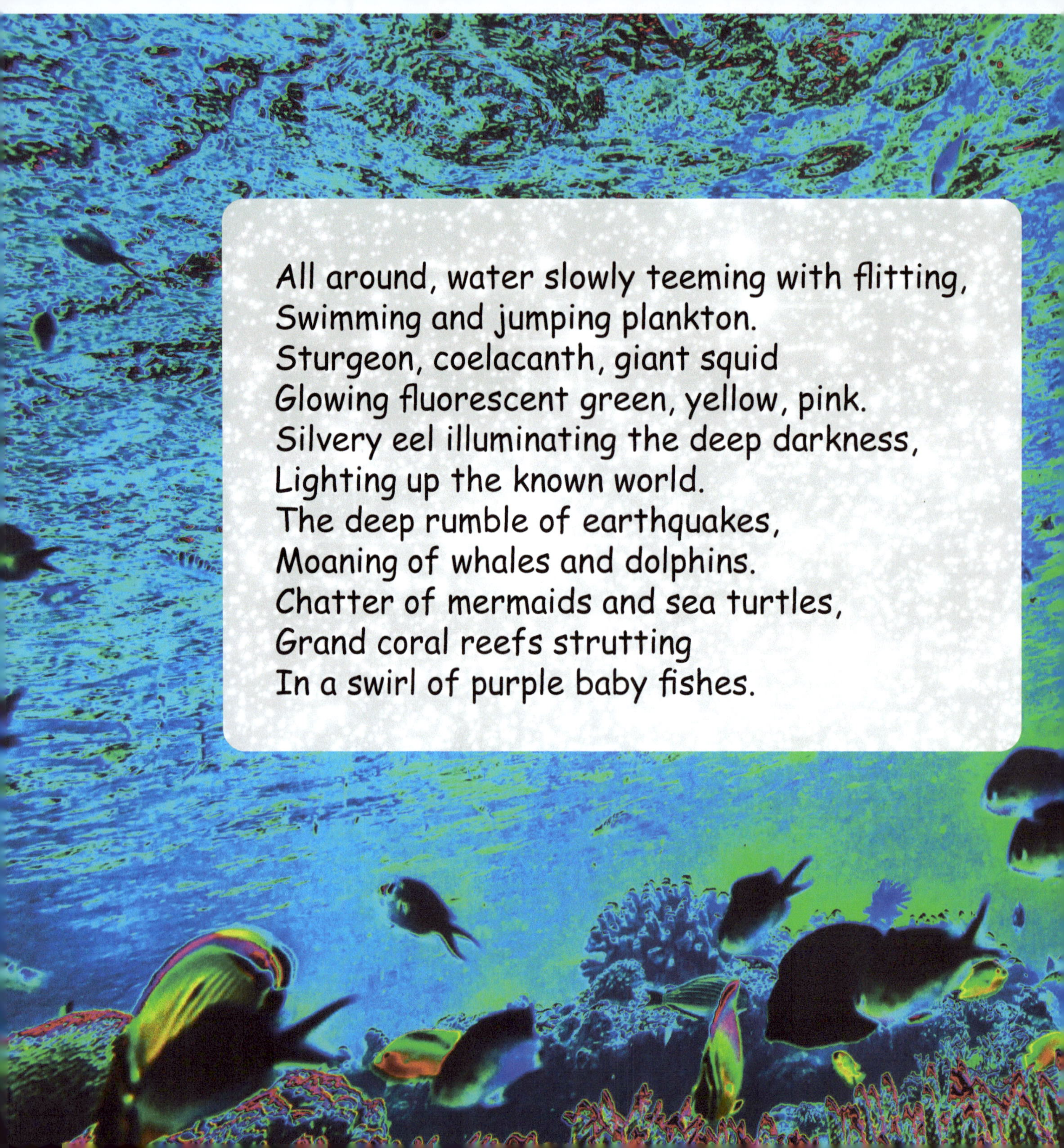
All around, water slowly teeming with flitting,
Swimming and jumping plankton.
Sturgeon, coelacanth, giant squid
Glowing fluorescent green, yellow, pink.
Silvery eel illuminating the deep darkness,
Lighting up the known world.
The deep rumble of earthquakes,
Moaning of whales and dolphins.
Chatter of mermaids and sea turtles,
Grand coral reefs strutting
In a swirl of purple baby fishes.

And then, Earth rebirthing and dying.
Again and again, the rumble and shaking.
Volcanos spewing tangerine smoke and gray ash, blocking sun.
An outer space boulder crashing, raising soil to the heavens,
Boiling the oceans, sending seven tsunamis.
Then fires, then no sun again, freezing and a great flood.
Vast, shrieking death of animal, plant and mineral.
Then life, then death, then life—above and below.

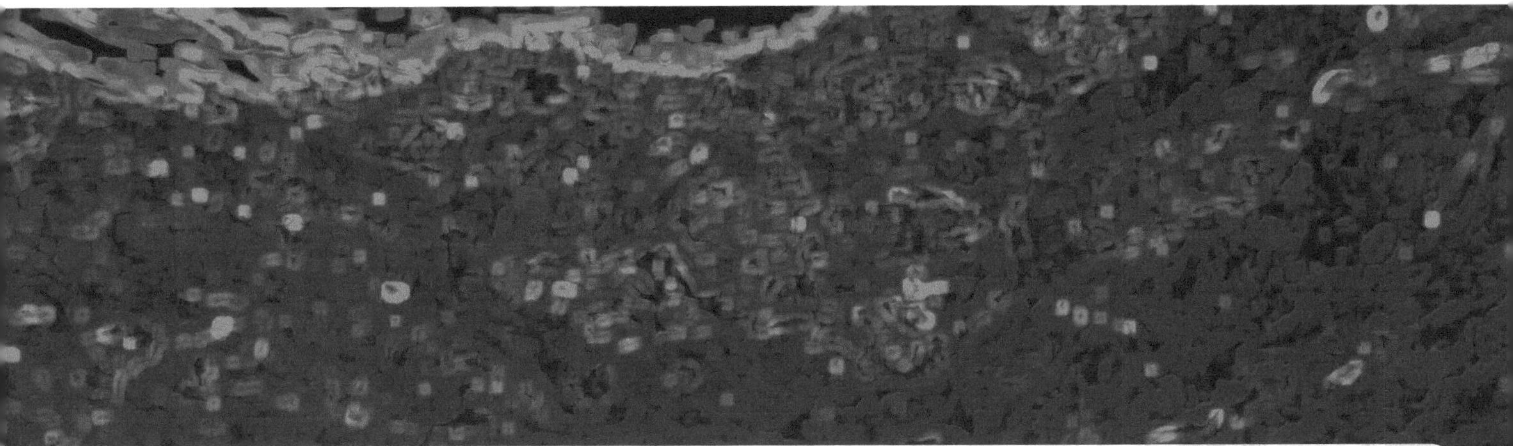

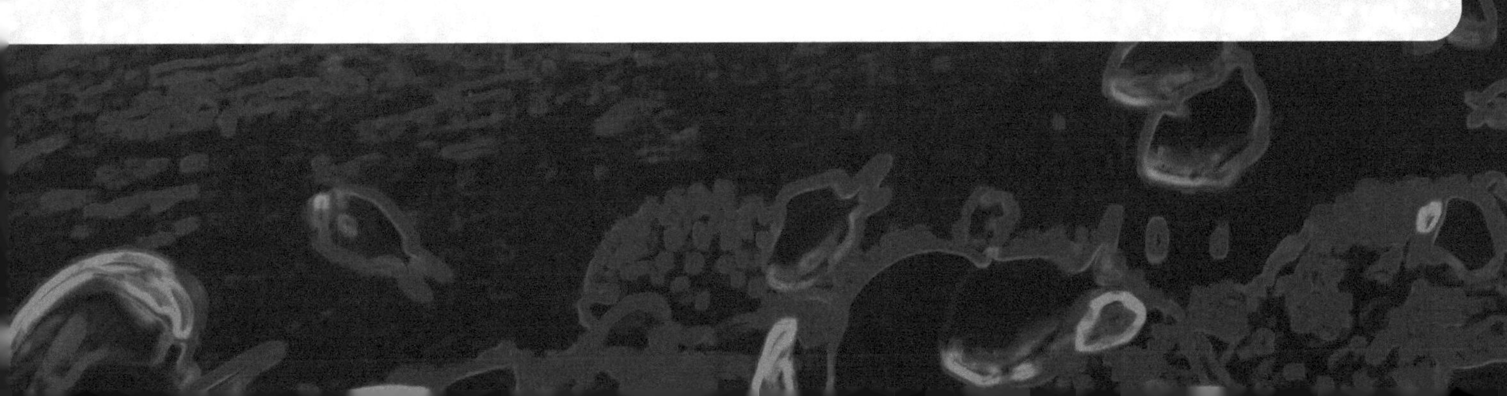

For millennia, hardly any humans on the ocean.
Then only a few boat bottoms visible way above.
Appearing as tiny almonds or floating paper
Outlined by flickering sunlight.
But it was fourteen centuries after Jesus, thirty centuries after
Giza stopped fueling crafts from distant galaxies
That wooden ships started crossing and re-crossing the Atlantic.
Food garbage, then human feces, then limbs, then entire corpses.
Jagged-edge skulls, tibia, fibula and pelvic bones,
Half consumed by sharks, barracudas and crustaceans.
Tiny remnants of human flesh fluttering to the depths like snow.

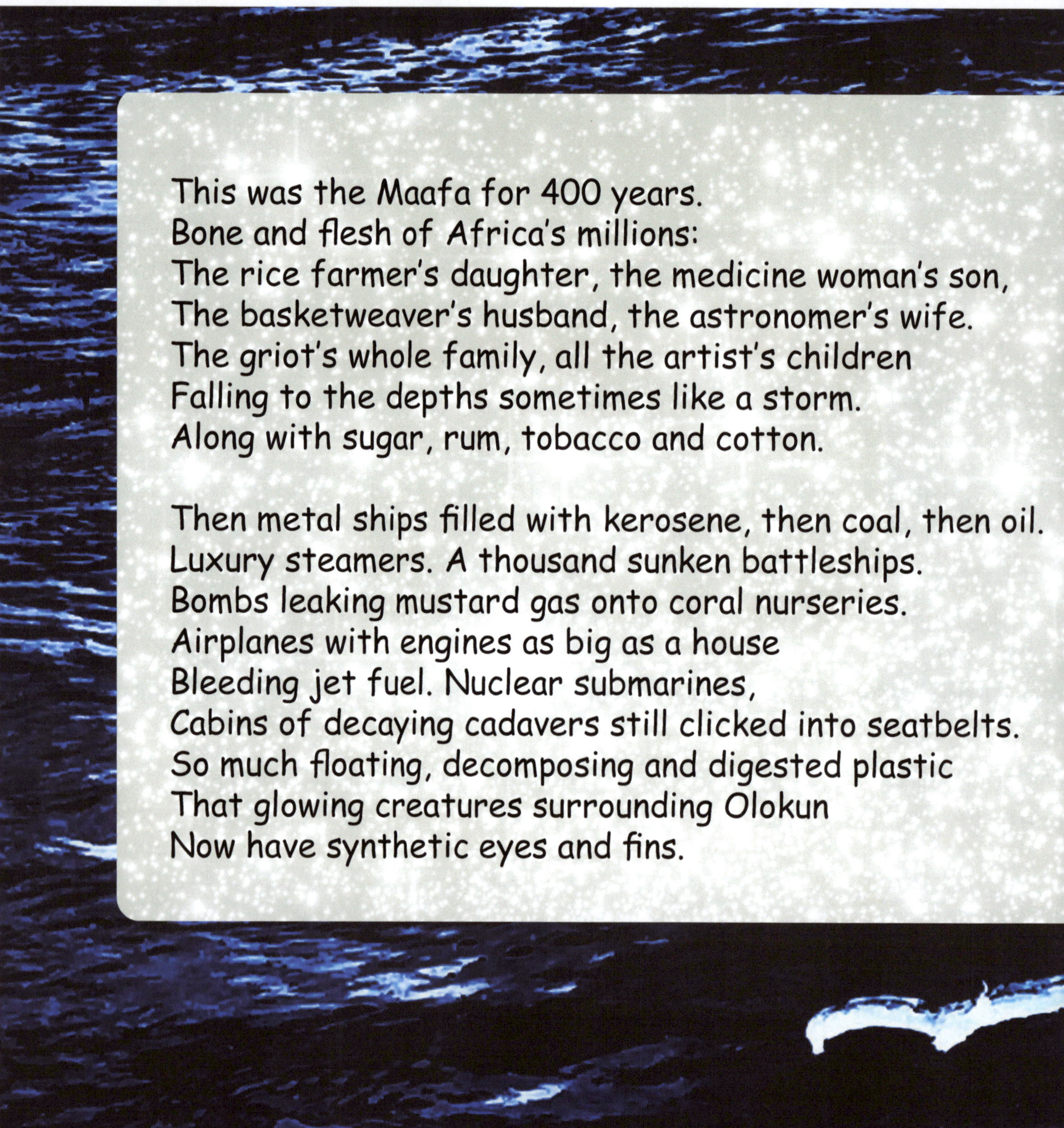

This was the Maafa for 400 years.
Bone and flesh of Africa's millions:
The rice farmer's daughter, the medicine woman's son,
The basketweaver's husband, the astronomer's wife.
The griot's whole family, all the artist's children
Falling to the depths sometimes like a storm.
Along with sugar, rum, tobacco and cotton.

Then metal ships filled with kerosene, then coal, then oil.
Luxury steamers. A thousand sunken battleships.
Bombs leaking mustard gas onto coral nurseries.
Airplanes with engines as big as a house
Bleeding jet fuel. Nuclear submarines,
Cabins of decaying cadavers still clicked into seatbelts.
So much floating, decomposing and digested plastic
That glowing creatures surrounding Olokun
Now have synthetic eyes and fins.

And just as satellites and space junk surround the earth,
An island of plastic floats in the Pacific,
The detritus and counter-proof of human progress,
Swirling at the end of the dying known world.
Earthquakes more and more.
Tsunamis rise on their hind legs.
The planet warms—above and below.

A new glow of methane slowly rises underneath Olokun.
Trapped there since the last great freeze and now escaping.
Olokun staves off the day when plankton gasp for oxygen.
For when the plankton die, oceans will blink out in darkness.

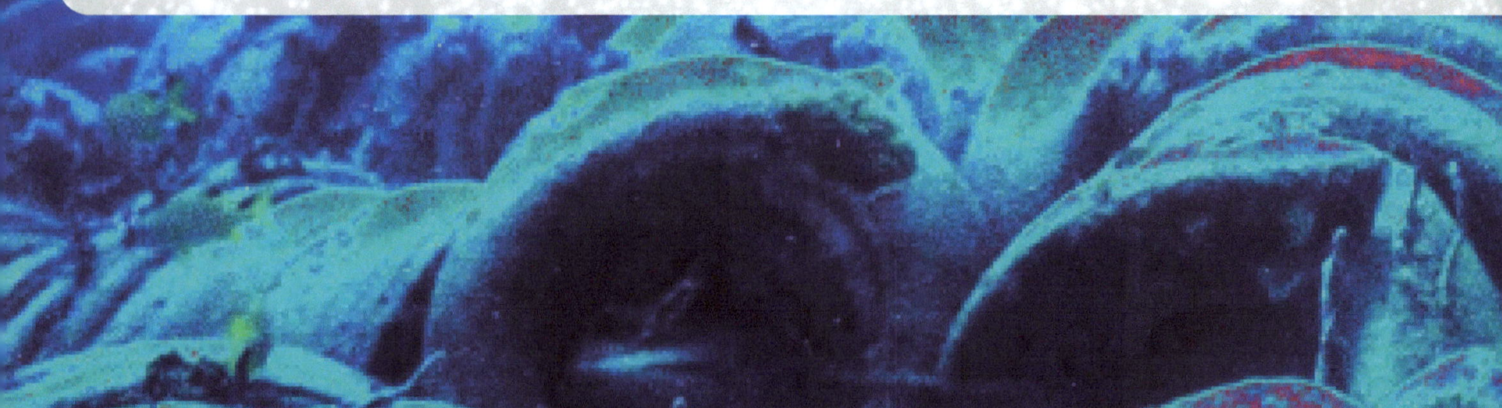

Earth's medicine is harsh but self-healing.
Slavers, pirates, warmongers and oil drillers
Only bow to destruction anyway.
Earth game recognize Earth game
That Olokun prays humans will survive.

Can monsoons cool oceans?
Can salt eat away dumped poisons?
Can tiny whirlpools spin out new oxygen?
Can plankton blink to reboot?
Can a passing wand of seaweed turn reefs
Green, yellow, pink and teeming again?
Olokun meets Oya. Ocean meets wind.
Their capes blowing behind them in the clouds.
Sending hurricanes to the land of Maafa.

600 years flutter down like a storm.
And Olokun has taken off into space.
Finding Olokun on other planets and moons!
They, too, carry souls of the Maafa,
Which is known throughout the galaxy.
Every lost sailor is known.
Every drowned refugee.
Every radioactive dagger from Fukushima.
All are signs of Hopi prophecy fulfilled:

Olokun for Titan

War destroys the land where humans received
"the first light of wisdom." And a web covers the earth,
Covers spoiled oceans, seas, rivers, creeks and lakes.
Olokun gazes from space on the tarnished blue marble
With love of and fear for foolish humans.

S/he lifts up those cleaning oceans and rivers,
Driving electric cars, buying composting toilets,
Choosing to walk and not fly, living with nature,
Rather than destroying it.
For water is life for all creatures above.
And water is life for all creatures below.

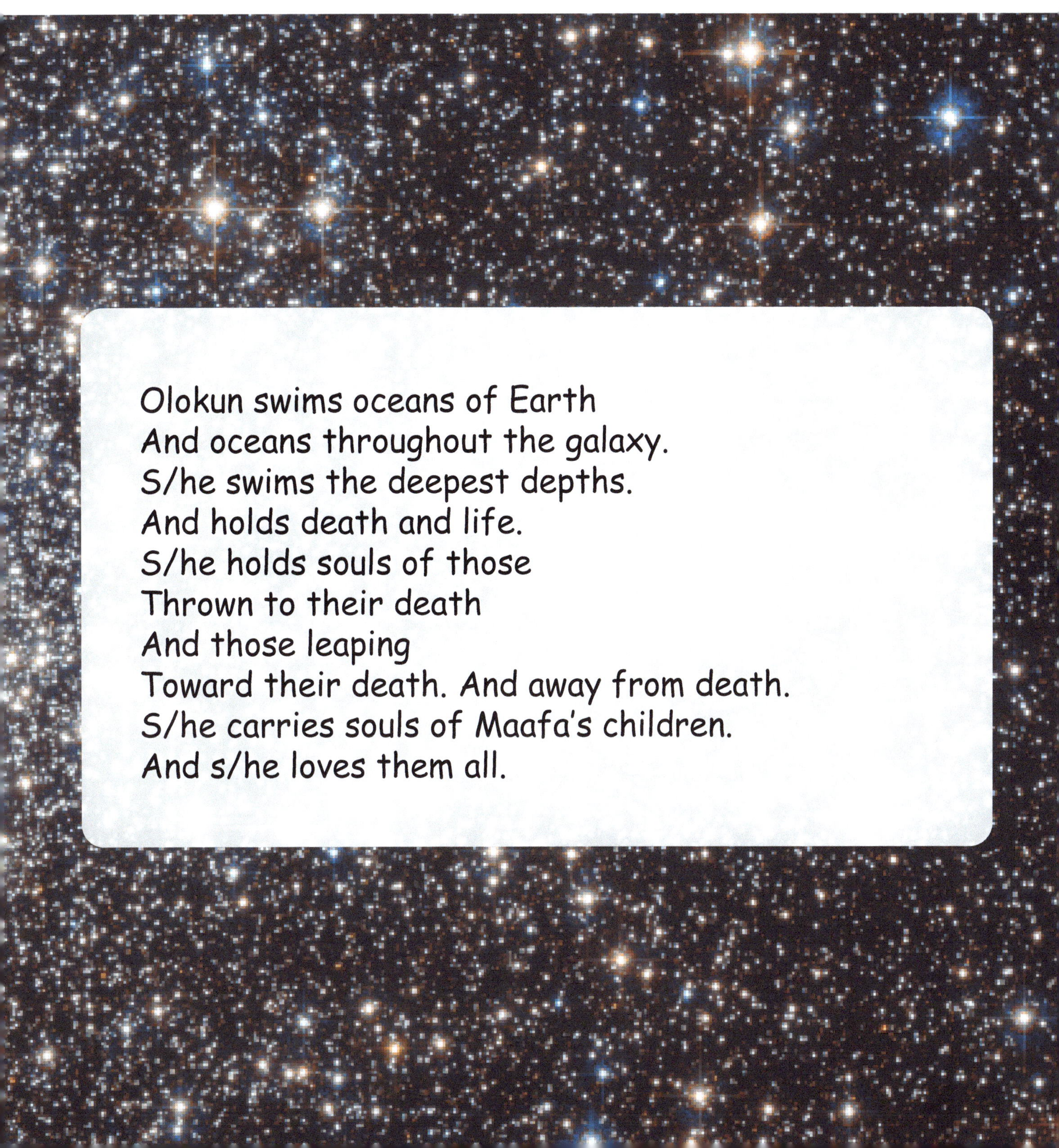

Olokun swims oceans of Earth
And oceans throughout the galaxy.
S/he swims the deepest depths.
And holds death and life.
S/he holds souls of those
Thrown to their death
And those leaping
Toward their death. And away from death.
S/he carries souls of Maafa's children.
And s/he loves them all.

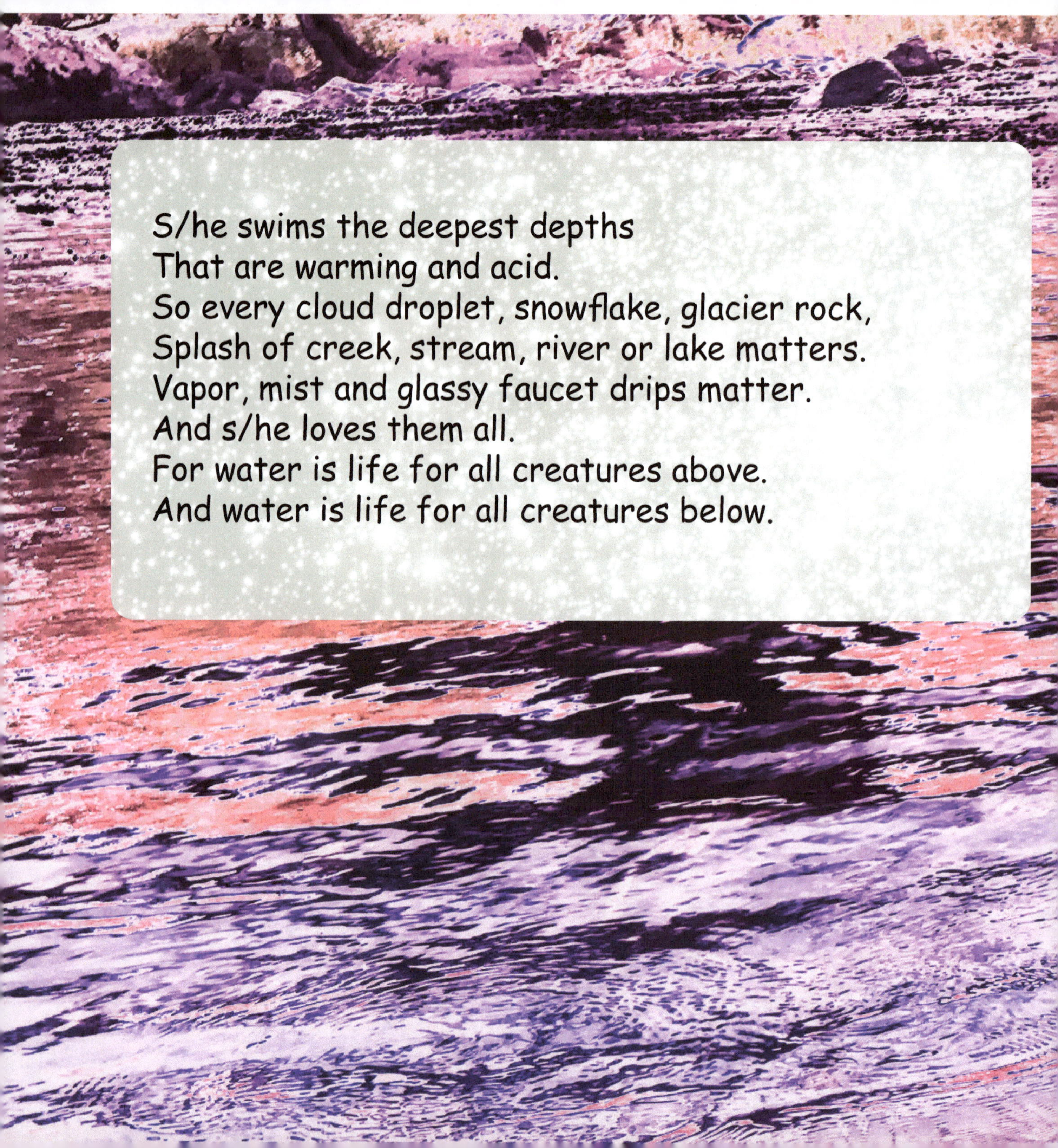

S/he swims the deepest depths
That are warming and acid.
So every cloud droplet, snowflake, glacier rock,
Splash of creek, stream, river or lake matters.
Vapor, mist and glassy faucet drips matter.
And s/he loves them all.
For water is life for all creatures above.
And water is life for all creatures below.

Epilogue:
Water Places in the Universe for Olokun:

Earth
Olokun's home is Earth, the rocky third planet from our sun. Two-thirds of Earth is covered by ocean water. Most of this ocean water is beyond the continental shelves, starting at 600 feet deep and plunging as deep as 36,000 feet. It is at these deepest depths where Olokun lives.

Mars
On the neighboring planet Mars, Olokun swims in secret underwater lakes that humans have yet to discover. In 2016, NASA discovered a large amount of underground ice on Mars with enough water to fill Lake Superior but they haven't yet discovered Olokun's swimming spot. Olokun is an old soul and s/he remembers when there was plenty of surface water on Mars, which is now gone, except for frozen water at its two polar caps.

Enceladus
What fun Olokun has riding geysers of water that erupt from this Saturn moon's underground ocean. Then Olokun returns to the ocean below the icy crust to take another geyser ride, kind of like being at a water park, or riding a cold version of Old Faithful, the geyser in Yellowstone Park. Olokun's swims on Enceladus are marathon because the subsurface ocean encircles the entire moon!

Titan

Olokun enjoys this Saturn moon's rivers, lakes and seas, which are filled with liquid methane rather than water. In fact, for a long time, Titan was the only planetary body other than earth known to have surface liquid. In addition to its surface liquid, it has a dense atmosphere (of nitrogen), with a cycle much like Earth's water cycle, so on Titan it does not rain water, it rains liquid methane!

Europa

Like Enceladus, Europa is covered with an icy crust so Olokun swims most beneath the surface where there is a large body of water. Also like Enceladus, Europa is known to have geysers and after the water erupts, it rains back down onto the surface, layering Europa's shiny surface.

Ganymede

Olokun may hop to this other Jupiter moon, Ganymede, to take a swim in its deep saline ocean that exists under 90 miles of ice.

Ceres

Ceres is one of the most unusual places in the galaxy for Olokun to live because it is not a planet like Earth, it is not a moon like Europa, Enceladus or Titan—it is an asteroid! Though it is made up of mainly rock and ice, Ceres also has an internal ocean of liquid water. Ceres is a huge asteroid, making up one-third the mass of the entire asteroid belt. It even has its own gravity. For Olokun, swimming on Ceres is like swimming in a pool on a cruise ship.

Olokun Places Outside our Solar System:
Thousands of planets outside of our solar system have been
discovered by humans since 2009 and many of these extrasolar
or "exoplanets" are in what is called the "habitable zone" in
relationship to their own sun—they are not too close to their sun to
be too hot and they are not too far away to be too cold. Of course,
Olokun knows all about these planets and these are some favorites:

Trappist-1 Seven Planets
What fun the Trappist-1 system is! Here, only 40 light years from
Earth, Olokun can hop from among seven planets that orbit close
to each other and can be seen in the sky from the surface of the
other planets. Olokun especially loves the oceans of three of the
planets and has many friends in the constellation Aquarius.

Gliese 1214b, 42 light years from Earth, is a planet covered
entirely by water with very little rocky land. When Gliese
1214b orbited in the habitable zone of its sun in the past, it
was a favorite place for Olokun because the water was a great
temperature. Now the planet has become hotter, best suited for
Olokun when s/he wants to sit in a very hot tub!

Kepler-22b is two and a half times the size of Earth, orbits
around a sun that is smaller than our sun and is located in
the constellation Cygnus—about 600 light years away. With
temperatures of about 72 degrees, Olokun finds Kepler-22b to be
a great place to relax and take in some mild rays.

GJ 504b, "the pink planet," in the constellation Virgo, 57 light years from Earth, has clouds made of frozen water droplets.

Other great spots! Kepler-1229b, Kapteynb, Kepler-442, Kepler-62f, Kepler-186f, Kepler-442b, GJ 667Cc, GJ667Cf and GJ667Ce.

Olokun is truly of the Milky Way Galaxy! Olokun says Black Lives Matter! Water is life! Mni Wicomi!

www.ingramcontent.com/pod-product-compliance
Lightning Source LLC
Chambersburg PA
CBHW041420300726
48981CB00007B/355